D0953193

TWO DOGS
IN A TRENCH COAT

Go on a Class Trip

TWO DOGS  TRENCH COAT

Go on a Class Trip

by Julie Falatko

Illustrated by Colin Jack

Scholastic Press / New York

Library of Congress Cataloging-in-Publication Data available

ISBN 978-1-338-18955-1

10 9 8 7 6 5 4 3 2 1   19 20 21 22 23

Printed in the U.S.A.   23
First edition, June 2019

Book design by Elizabeth B. Parisi

For Ramona, Zuzu, Eli, and Henry:
Thanks for going to all those museums with me.

CHAPTER ONE

Waldo was looking forward to having two **lunches**, or maybe three.

He knew he was going to have more than one **lunch** because his teacher, Ms. Twohey, had just handed him a piece of paper that said *Field Trip Permission Slip* at the top, and there was an exciting section called **Lunch** and there was a check box for **Bag Lunch** and a check box for **Home Lunch**.

Waldo was going to check both those boxes. He was also wondering what would happen if he drew more squares and put check marks in those too. Would he get two dozen **lunches**?

"We might get two dozen **lunches**," Waldo whispered to Sassy.

"Finally, enough **food**," said Sassy. She was a big dog with impressive cheeks, who was wondering about the very important forms their teacher was giving everyone. Sassy couldn't see the form herself because she was sitting under Waldo at their desk in their classroom.

"I should get half those **lunches**," said Sassy, "so pass me twenty of them."

"I will pass them to you in just a minute," Waldo whispered back, "or maybe tomorrow. As soon as I get all the **lunches**, you will get approximately half of them."

Every school day the dogs stacked themselves up and put on a trench coat, then walked into Bea Arthur Memorial Elementary School and Learning Commons and pretended to be a human student named Salty.

It was a pretty good trick. They had started going to school to make sure everything was okay with their boy, Stewart. It was. Now they kept going to school because school was so fun. They had **lunch** every day, got to spend more time with Stewart and all their new human friends, learned math and reading, and did fun activities like recess and clubs and **snack**.

"Class, it's time to talk about our field trip tomorrow," said Ms. Twohey.

Waldo raised his paw. "**Yes, let's talk about it**," said Waldo. "**What is a field trip? Is it running a lot in a field?**"

"A field trip is when we leave school grounds for additional educational opportunities," said Ms. Twohey, "not when we run in a field."

"**I am from Liver, Ohio**," said Waldo.

"Technically," said a boy named Ralph, "we could go on a field trip to a field."

"Aw, I wish we went to a field," said Salty's good friend Bax. "That would be awesome."

"Unfortunately," said Ms. Twohey, "there is no edu-cational field in our area, so we will visit the City Museum."

The students all groaned.

"We go there every year!" said Stewart.

"That may be true," said Ms. Twohey. "But I think you'll find as you get older that you get more and more out of our fantastic local museum."

Waldo tilted his head to the side. "I like looking at cows," he said.

"Cows?" said Ms. Twohey.

"Right," said Waldo. "Isn't that what you said? Cows? At the Moo-see-em?"

"Good one!" said Bax.

Ms. Twohey explained to Salty that the City Museum held a variety of learning-oriented exhibits about history, paleontology, geology, astronomy, biology, and art. They would be spending the entire day there instead of going to school.

She wrote a list on the board.

"These are the things you need to remember to bring for tomorrow," she said. "Your completed packet of forms. **Lunch** and a **snack**, if you're bringing those from home. Comfortable walking shoes. And an attentive and positive mind that is ready to learn!"

"**My mind is also ready to eat!**" said Waldo.

"And remember," continued Ms. Twohey, "you must obey the rules and follow all museum regulations and field trip protocol. If you behave appropriately, you will get an **ice cream** party. If you misbehave, no **ice cream**."

"**I want ice cream!**" said Waldo.

"Sure you do," said Ms. Twohey. "So do I. And those of you who follow all the rules tomorrow will get a Good Job sticker *and* an **ice cream** party. I know I'm going to follow all the rules tomorrow. You won't find me engaging in any shenanigans!"

"Are shenanigans like **butterscotch sauce**?" asked Waldo.

"No," said Ms. Twohey.

CHAPTER TWO

I am going to have two **lunches**," said Waldo. "Or maybe five."

"What do you mean?" asked Stewart.

Stewart and the dogs had just arrived at home. Waldo, Sassy, and Stewart ran in circles in the backyard for a few minutes. Then Stewart sat on the back steps and took the field trip forms out of his backpack. Waldo and Sassy looked over his shoulder.

"I am going to check all the boxes," said Waldo.

"Half of those **lunch boxes** are mine," said Sassy.

"I'm pretty sure you're only supposed to check one box," said Stewart.

"But Ms. Twohey talks about going above and beyond, and I am going to do that by checking more than one box."

"You can try," said Stewart. "How are you going to get parental permission to go on the field trip? Do I have to pretend to be your parent?"

Sassy yawned. "That's ridiculous. You're not our parent. You're our boy."

"We will give ourselves permission," said Waldo. "A dog is self-parenting."

"But I feed you and walk you and stuff," said Stewart. "Because you're my dogs."

"You do that because you're our boy," said Sassy.

"It's our job to protect you," said Waldo.

"Kind of like a parent," said Sassy.

"Yes!" said Waldo. "That is true! I will sign your parental percussion form."

"Thanks," said Stewart. "But I can get my parents to do that. You know, my human parents."

"They do love to sign forms," said Waldo.

Waldo pulled the field trip forms out of his backpack and looked over them, a pencil in his paw.

"This is fun!" he said. "Yes, we will be good. No, we will not write on the art. Yes, we will bring home **lunch** *and* get box **lunch**. Yes. We will behave. Yes. Yes. Hmmm."

"What's wrong?" asked Sassy.

"There are a lot of rules," said Waldo.

"They're pretty basic things," said Stewart.

"It's so many rules. I don't think I can memorize all these rules in time. I work best when I'm told one rule and given a **cookie** every time I remember it. Then I can go on to a new rule. This is four pages of rules that I need to know by tomorrow."

"You don't need to memorize all of them," said Stewart.

"There are rules about touching things and rules about elephants and fountains. There are rules about **bananas**."

"There aren't **banana** rules. Seriously, you only need to remember not to destroy any of the museum displays," said Stewart. "You can remember that."

"Can I?" said Waldo. "I'm a dog. Sometimes I destroy priceless museum displays."

"No, you don't."

"Just last week I ripped up that bag you brought home."

"That was **leftovers** from a restaurant," said Stewart. "Which I was bringing home for you to eat anyway."

"Still, it was beautiful, and I destroyed it."

"What if I *have* to chew on an antique rug?" asked Sassy. "That happens sometimes."

"Should we . . . should we chew on the rug in the living room to get any rug chewing out of our systems?" asked Waldo.

"Yes," said Sassy.

"No," said Stewart. "Listen, you're overthinking all this. You'll be fine. It's just a long, boring day at the same old museum."

"You smell like you're not happy about the field trip tomorrow," said Waldo.

"We do this same field trip to the City Museum every year," said Stewart. "We see the same exhibits every year. It's the same dinosaurs, statues, and dusty animal dioramas every year."

"And you are sad because the animals have dust?" said Sassy.

"Ms. Twohey is a good teacher," said Waldo. "Doesn't she make the field trip fun? She said we get **ice cream**! And a sticker!"

"Ms. Twohey doesn't lead us on City Museum day," said Stewart. "The tour guides do, and they're the worst. The tour guides always have this idea that, because we're kids, they have to talk down to us. They talk to us like we're babies. It's awful. But Ms. Twohey loves the tour guides because she says that they dispense so much educational information."

"You should stage a kid rebellion where you overthrow the grown-ups!" said Waldo, wagging his tail. "Then you could get us more **snacks**."

"I'm not sure those things are related," said Stewart.

"So it's going to be a boring day?" said Sassy. "Are there any good places to nap?"

"Not really. It's all cold stone," said Stewart.

"Cold stone with a doggy bed on top?" asked Sassy.

"Nope," said Stewart.

"Maybe it will be all different this year?" said Waldo.

"Sometimes there are new exhibits, but it's impossible to get excited about them because of the way the tour guide talks to us. And we can't even have fun on our own. One year we tried to do a scavenger hunt, but the museum guards caught us and made everyone go back to the tour." Stewart stood and stretched. "I'm going to go get us a **snack**."

"That is a good idea," said Waldo. "Keep our strength up for tomorrow."

The dogs watched Stewart go into the house.

"Our boy does not want to go to the museum tomorrow," said Sassy. "Should I eat his permission form?"

"Maybe," said Waldo. "I do not want to be bored all day."

"With no place to nap."

"And all these rules to memorize."

"But I do want dozens of **lunches**," said Sassy.

"And if we're good, we get an **ice cream** party," said Waldo.

"I want **ice cream**," said Sassy.

"It is settled," said Waldo. "We will go on the field trip tomorrow. We will remember all the rules and also all the new facts about the museum. We will not eat any priceless artifacts. We will have two **lunches**. And we'll save Stewart from boredom."

CHAPTER THREE

The next morning, Waldo was in a tizzy getting ready for the field trip.

"How much **food** do I need? Should I bring a compass? Do I need a sleeping bag? Do I need to tell the lady who brings the mail?"

"What would you need to tell the postal carrier?" asked Stewart.

"Are we moving?" asked Waldo.

"What?"

"To the City Museum."

"No," said Stewart.

"And is now a good time for me to tell you I feel hungry?" asked Sassy.

"I just gave you **breakfast**," said Stewart. "Plus aren't you always hungry?"

"But it's a feel trip," said Sassy. "So I should tell you how I feel."

"I also feel hungry," said Waldo. "How do you feel, Stewart?"

"I feel bored already in anticipation of a day of boredom," said Stewart. "But at least you both will be there."

Waldo finished stuffing his backpack with a stack of index cards, a **sandwich**, and as many **baby carrots** as he could fit.

When they got to school, most of their class was already crowded around tables that were set up on the front lawn near a school bus. Coach, the gym teacher, was there, blowing on his whistle, corralling everyone into lines. Ms. Twohey was running from the bus to the school to the children, carrying tote bags, water bottles, and cardboard boxes of bagged **lunch**.

"Oh, look! It is a box of bags of **lunch**!" said Waldo. "That's fun! I hope I am allowed to have as much **lunch** as I can stuff in my pockets."

First everyone had to stop by one table to turn in their field trip permission forms. The bag **lunches** were at the next table, and everyone who ordered a **lunch** picked one up there and put it into their backpack. Waldo accidentally ate half of the **sandwich** when he stuck his nose into the bag to smell what was in there. Sassy noticed, and so Waldo dropped the other half of the **sandwich** onto the ground for her. Good thing they had two **lunches**, since **lunch** number one was already gone and the school day hadn't even really started yet.

The third table had bright red bandanas with the Bea Arthur Memorial Elementary School logo on them.

"Here is your bandana. Make sure you put it on," said Dottie, the school secretary.

"This is not my **banana**," said Waldo. "I thought we were getting two **lunches**, a **snack**, and a **banana**."

"No, these are so everyone knows you're part of the school's group," said Dottie. "These are to make sure you don't get lost."

"We **might get lost**?" said Waldo.

"Not if you wear this bandana," said Dottie.

"Lost?" Waldo whispered down to Sassy. "No wonder Stewart does not like the museum."

"We'll make sure we stay close to him," said Sassy.

Stewart came over and helped Waldo tie the bandana around his neck.

"It's a very handsome **banana** but not the kind you eat," said Waldo. "I **look jaunty**." He took out his index cards.

"Whatcha got there?" asked Bax.

"I made flash cards to help me remember all the rules," said Waldo. "There are so many rules. This is the **banana** rule: 'Every student must wear a school **banana** so they are clearly identified as Bea Arthur Memorial Elementary School students.' Did you know about that rule?"

"Sure," said Bax. "The bandana's probably the most interesting thing that happens on the whole field trip. Which isn't saying much."

Coach blew his whistle three times and handed Ms. Twohey a megaphone.

"I'm glad to see you're all here and ready for an exciting and enriching day of learning at the City Museum!" said Ms. Twohey. "Remember, the most important thing is to follow all the rules. That will ensure a successful trip."

"You said the rules weren't important!" Waldo whispered to Stewart.

"They're not," said Stewart. "Or, I mean, they are, but they're really no big deal. Don't destroy anything, don't run around, and don't get lost."

"Any questions?" said Ms. Twohey.

"MS. Twohey! MS. Twohey!" said Waldo, raising his paw. "I do not want to get lost."

"That's right, Salty," said Ms. Twohey. "Good job."

Sassy sat down suddenly so no one would see her tail wagging. She liked being told she was doing a good job. If they did a good job all day, they'd get **ice cream**. She hoped Waldo would give her all the **ice cream**. He should. She held him up all day. She should get all the **ice cream**.

"Everyone! It's time to get on the bus!" said Ms. Twohey.

"I have never been on a bus!" said Waldo.

"What, really?" asked Bax. "How is that possible?"

"I am from Liver, Ohio."

"Huh," said Bax. "Well, no big deal. It's just a bus."

It wasn't just a bus though. It was a school bus. Every dog wanted to catch a particular set of vehicles: a dump truck, a trash truck, a mail truck, and a school bus.

"Does it count as catching it if we go inside it?" Waldo asked Sassy.

"It's even better," said Sassy.

Salty walked down the aisle of the bus and sat down next to Stewart. Ms. Twohey was the last one on. She walked down the aisle and checked students off on a checklist on her clipboard.

She leaned out the door of the bus. "Coach, whistle us out!"

Coach blew a series of short blasts on his whistle to alert everyone around to the bus's departure, and they were off.

CHAPTER FOUR

I LOVE RIDING ON A BUS!" shouted Waldo.

It was true: Riding on a bus was even more fun than the dogs expected it to be. The warm floor and the way the bus bumped down the road lulled Sassy into a deep sleep in less than a minute. Stewart moved so the dogs could have the window seat.

"I wonder what this little latch does," said Waldo, pawing at the window until it slid open. He stuck his head out. "Wheeeee!"

"Hey, that looks fun," said Bax, who also stuck his head out a window.

Then all the other students saw how much fun they were having, and they stuck their heads out the window too. Ms. Twohey was glad everyone was so excited about the field trip to the City Museum that they were sticking their heads out of the bus window to get a better look at it as they approached.

The bus parked and the students streamed off.

"Oh! Here he is! Hooray!" Ms. Twohey was bouncing. "Gordy! Gordy! Over here!"

A man waved and jogged over to the students. He was wearing a light green shirt tucked into tan pants, and was holding something behind his back.

"Well, there they all are!" he said, in a singsong voice that sounded like he was imitating a circus clown and a cartoon rabbit. "Who wants to guess what I have behind my back?"

"A hat," said the students, using their most lackluster voices.

"That's right, a hat!" said Gordy, pulling a white hat out and putting it on his head. "And do you know what kind of hat this is, kiddos? A ship captain's hat! Yessirree! Righty-o! And why do you think I'm wearing a ship captain's hat?"

"Because you're the captain of this tour," said the kids in a bored monotone.

"Golly gosh oh gee you are a bunch of smarty-pants, aren't you? A three-hour tour, right? Ha ha ha."

No one laughed.

"Are we going on a boat?" asked Waldo.

"No, but we'll see a boat," said Gordy.

"What is the ship you are captaining?" asked Waldo.

"The ship," said Gordy, placing a hand on Waldo's shoulder and pointing toward the sky, "is YOU."

"I am not a ship."

"No, this tour! The whole darn lot of you! You're the ship that I'll steer through the artifacts and mysteries of time! Now kidderoonies, are you ready?"

No one answered. Bax was sitting cross-legged on the grass, head resting on his hand, eyes closed. Arden was looking intently at her thumbnail. Becky squinted at something in the distance.

"I said," said Gordy, louder. "Are you ready?"

"I guess we're ready," said Stewart.

"I am ready to save Stewart," said Waldo.

"I am ready to save Stewart *and* have an **ice cream** party," said Sassy.

"Yeah, sure, I'm ready," said Bax, groaning as he pushed himself up off the ground.

"Then let's set sail on an adventure through HISTORY!" said Gordy, who turned around and ran up the steps to the big front doors of the City Museum. Ms. Twohey bounded up the stairs after him.

"This is always the most exciting day of the year!" said Ms. Twohey. "To be able to see all the wonderful exhibits in the City Museum! And to be showed around by such a vivacious guide! It's inspiring."

Ralph yawned.

Waldo made sure his bandana was secure. He made sure he had his backpack and his index cards with all the rules. "Pay attention to the tour guide," he read from a card.

"You are paying too much attention to the tour guide and not enough to finding us twelve extra **lunches**," said Sassy.

Gordy held the door open and ushered the students in. A security guard stood just inside the door, glaring. She wore a navy-blue sweater and had a walkie-talkie clipped on to her waistband.

The room they entered was huge. The ceiling was as high as four elementary schools stacked on top of each other, and the walls

were so wide you could lay one thousand German shep-
herds end to end from one wall to the other. Sassy felt
an immense desire to run in large looping circles
around that room, and she had to concentrate very
hard to stay still in one spot. Some sort of gigantic
snake hung from the ceiling.

"The Hall of Enormity!" said Gordy. "Where our
journey begins! Okay, kiddies, let's get ready to begin
the most fantastic—"

"What is that snake?" asked Waldo. "Stewart, I am sure you are not bored when there is a giant, possibly evil snake looming above our heads!"

"It's the same old huge snake that they always have in the lobby," said Stewart.

"Will it eat us?" said Waldo.

"Will it serve us **lunch**?" said Sassy.

"That majestic creature up there," said Gordy, "is a megasnakus paleoslitheradon."

"Technically," said Ralph, "that's a fake dinosaur."

"But it's based on a real dinosaur," said Gordy.

"Right, but technically, that one never existed," said Ralph.

"It's an artist's rendering," said Gordy. "A lot of ancient creatures were fantastic gigantics! There was a guinea pig the size of a golf cart and a penguin that was taller than me."

"I would not like to see a squirrel that is a bigger size than a dog. Is there one of those?" Waldo asked.

"No, silly billies, it's just an example of the sorts of things we have here!" said Gordy. "We have historical artifacts *and* we have art, and sometimes the two are combined, like in that megasnake up there. Okay. Enough of that. It's time for us to go to our very first exhibit: outer space!"

CHAPTER FIVE

D o you think we'll go to space in a spaceship?" whispered Sassy.

"The real question is whether or not we'll be able to stick our heads out of the spaceship windows so we can smell space flying by," Waldo whispered back.

The students walked down a cold stone hall to a doorway with *The Wonders of Space* written on the wall above it.

The room was very dark. The children bumped into each other for a moment before Gordy turned on a flashlight.

"Hey, keep that light off in here!" shouted a guard standing against the wall. "You'll ruin the ambience."

"Maybe if the ambience in this exhibit wasn't *completely pitch-black* I wouldn't need to," said Gordy.

"The old 'guards versus guides' rivalry strikes again," said Bax.

"**What is that you are talking about**?" asked Waldo.

"The museum guards and the tour guides don't get along," explained Stewart. "The guards think the guides are loudmouth show-offs, and the guides think the guards are muscle-bound enforcers who are always looking for people breaking the rules."

"Who is right?" said Waldo.

"I guess they both are," said Stewart.

"It's like Afghan hounds versus basset hounds," said Waldo.

"What's that?" said Bax.

"What?" said Waldo.

"Huh?" said Bax.

The centerpiece of the room was a meteorite about the size of a loaf of **bread**. It stood on a golden pedestal, with a shaft of light directed down on it from the ceiling.

"That **bread** has gone bad," said Waldo. "But I will eat it if I must."

"Are you eating up there? Don't finish the **lunches** without me!" said Sassy.

"Don't eat that," whispered Stewart.

"All right, everyone, gather round," said Gordy.

"Why is he using a scary movie voice?" whispered Sassy.

"I think he's trying to be dramatic," said Stewart.

The kids all stepped one centimeter closer to Gordy. Some of them took advantage of the dark room to lie in a corner and take a nap. Ms. Twohey clapped her hands in glee and stood right in front of Gordy.

"Many years ago," said Gordy, "people thought the stars were evil monsters who were telling them stories."

"No," said Ralph under his breath. "Not quite."

"What *is* all that dark, dark space up there?" said Gordy. "There are people called *astronomers* who make it their job to find out the secrets of the giant mysteries of space. Can you all say that? It's a big word, I know! But give it a try! I know you can do it!"

"Astronomers!" said Ms. Twohey.

"Space," said the students, yawning.

Gordy led Ms. Twohey over to an illuminated poster on the wall. The rest of the class stayed where they were.

"That man talks to us like we're puppies, Stewart," said Waldo.

"I know. And we've all seen this so many times. I think outer space is really cool," said Stewart. "But Gordy makes it so boring."

Waldo decided that going over the rules might cheer Stewart up.

"Stewart, let's look at my rules cards some more," said Waldo. "That's fun! When you follow the rules, you get a **treat**, and if we follow these rules, we'll get **ice cream**. Which is the third best **treat**."

"What are the first and second best **treats**?" asked Stewart.

"First is a big pile of **hamburgers**," said Sassy.

"Second is **sausages**," said Waldo.

"**Ice cream** is three," said Sassy.

"Which I already said," said Waldo. "Number four is **cheese**."

"Number five is **carrots**," said Sassy.

"Really? **Carrots**?" said Stewart.

"That's just how it is," said Waldo. "It's not like we are making this up."

"We literally made it all up," said Sassy.

"How long is the list?" asked Stewart.

"Three hundred **treats** long," said Waldo.

Waldo took out his index cards.

"**Do not run**," he read. No one was running. Most of the students weren't even standing.

"**Do not touch the artwork**," he read. No one was touching anything. Although Waldo still wondered if he should eat that moldy space **bread**.

"Always wear your **banana**," he read.

Bax smiled. "Yeah, that's the spirit. Wear that **banana**!"

"Stay with the group," read Waldo.

"Here we are," said Arden, sighing. "In a group."

"The best part about space is astronaut **ice cream**," said Bax.

"I love **ice cream** with **nuts** in it," said Waldo.

"It doesn't have **nuts** in it," said Bax.

"You said it. Astronuts."

"I can show you some astronaut **ice cream** when we get to the gift shop," said Stewart.

Gordy was walking back toward the door, still talking to Ms. Twohey. "...and that's how Galileo changed everything!" he was saying.

"Wasn't that so fascinating, everyone?" said Ms. Twohey.

"What are those boots over there?" asked Waldo, pointing at a pair of silver boots with very thick soles on top of a pedestal.

"When I was a puppy I had a squeaky toy shaped like boots!" shout-whispered Sassy. "I chewed them until they were in shreds! I loved those boots so much!"

"Oh yeah, I remember those," said Stewart. "I don't think you had them for very long before you destroyed them."

"I had them for eight minutes," said Sassy.

"Those are rocket-powered astro-boots!" said Gordy. "They were designed so that astronauts could fly around space outside their rocket ship, or zoom around the moon!"

"When are you going to leave already?" said the

guard, walking toward the group. "Your flashlight antics are really killing our vibe."

"It's time for the Fantastic Jurassic!" said Gordy, backing quickly out the door. "Are you ready to go visit some giant dinos, kiddos?"

"Technically, a lot of the dinosaurs on display here were from the Cretaceous period," said Ralph.

"Heeeeeeere weeeeeeeeee go!" shouted Gordy, bounding out of the outer space exhibit.

"Okay, that was not very exciting," said Waldo, "but we will not give up. We can make the next room super fun."

"Good luck," said Stewart.

CHAPTER SIX

"Can you feel it, kids?" said Gordy, walking backward down the hall and facing Ms. Twohey. "Can you feel how we're going *back in time*?"

"No," said Bax.

"I do not want to go back in time!" Waldo whispered to Stewart. "I like chasing the squirrels and eating school **lunch** in this time!"

"We're not really going back in time," said Stewart.

"That is a huge relief."

The students followed Gordy down another big hall to an extra-wide doorway that was framed in giant bones. Enormous bones. Truly gigantic bones. Sassy had had a dream once where she found a secret door in the house she had never noticed before, and when she opened it, she saw a room filled with the biggest bones ever. Those dream bones were about half the size of the bones around the doorway.

"What is happ— How is— Stewart. What. I. Bones. Big bones." Waldo had temporarily forgotten how to put words together.

"Oh, just wait," said Stewart.

They walked through the bone door into the most amazing display of bones the dogs had ever seen. Bones the size of trees. Bones high above their heads. Bones right in front of their faces. All of them in the shapes of dinosaurs. They were, in fact, dinosaur bones.

"Stewart! Guess what?" said Waldo. "Nothing is boring anymore! This is the best day of my life now!"

"Don't be scared, kiddos!" said Gordy. "These dinos aren't going to come alive! They were alive millions of years ago!"

Waldo walked over to the biggest dinosaur in the room. Its head stretched almost to the ceiling. Each of its toe bones was as long as Waldo. Waldo remembered the rules. He did not run to the dinosaur. He did not shout at the dinosaur. He *did* lean over to smell the dinosaur. A tiny sniff.

"The dinosaur smells like bored children, dirty feet, cold stone floors, and mummies," Waldo said to Sassy. Waldo realized that was how the City Museum smelled in general.

"The most important thing is that it smells like dinosaur bones," said Sassy. "Which is my new favorite smell."

He would have to get closer to the dinosaur. It was important that he smelled it. It was his job. That was how he could be a good student. He could smell it, and learn so much. Ms. Twohey would be so proud of him that they would definitely have the **ice cream** party.

Waldo leaned way over, until his nose was resting on the ankle of the dinosaur. He breathed in deeply.

The dinosaur smelled like dirt from long ago, plaster, and a distant **meat** that Waldo found to be especially intriguing. Sassy could smell it too. It wasn't fair that Waldo always got to smell things out in the open, and she had to filter all the smells through both the trench coat and Waldo's back paws, which were on her head. She should be allowed to smell the dinosaur up close too.

Sassy peeked out of the trench coat. Ms. Twohey and Gordy were deep in conversation near a three-horned dinosaur skeleton on the other side of the room. The students still seemed bored, shockingly. Who could be bored in a room full of dinosaur bones?

Most of the class was sitting on the floor now. Stewart was next to Sassy, staring at the ceiling. Sassy tentatively put one paw on the raised platform that the immense dinosaur skeleton was affixed to. No one said anything, so she put her other front paw up there, and hoisted herself up. Now Salty was standing on the platform right next to all those tremendous bones.

"That was good thinking, Sassy," whispered Waldo. "Now we can study these bones up close."

"We're learning so much," Sassy whispered back.

The dogs both sniffed deeply, cataloging all the smells of the bones and the museum. Old paint, old clay, old metal, and old **lunch**. So many very old and fascinating smells.

It was clear what had to happen next. When smelling was good, tasting was better. You could really get the full bouquet of an object by tasting it. That was just common sense. That was smart. That was the best way to learn the facts.

Sassy took a step even closer to the leg of the dinosaur. Before they had been resting their noses on the bones, but now they could lean gently against them.

Waldo looked around. A few students were playing hangman and folding fortune-tellers. Piper was lying on her back, eyes closed. Ms. Twohey and Gordy were facing the opposite wall, looking at a time line of when different dinosaurs lived. Now was probably the best time to be a very good student and do some extra credit, in-depth investigative dinosaur tasting.

Waldo and Sassy both licked the ankle of the dinosaur tentatively. A feeling came over both dogs, an ancient instinct, the drive of their paleodog ancestors who hunted whopping creatures across vast, undeveloped plains with no comfy pillows or bowls of **kibble**.

Waldo and Sassy opened their mouths in unison and delicately wrapped their jaws around the lower leg of the dinosaur. It felt great. Triumphant. Delicious.

It made Waldo dreamy.

"We have caught the huge beast after running so fast. We won! And now we will drag the dinosaur through the field and the forest, near the park and down the street, until we bring it to our cave people family and it will be **dinner** for one million weeks," said Waldo.

Dinner. Yes. Maybe first they should chew on it.

Just a little bit.

Yes.

This is what it was like to be a dog from long ago, a dog who didn't have a basket of toys in the living room (or baskets, or toys, or a living room). A dog who chewed on a dinosaur surely lived in a cave and got rocks

instead of tennis balls. It was a hard life. But it was also a life where you got to chew on dinosaur bones. So that was nice.

"Dinosaur bones are better than **kibble**," said Waldo with a mouthful of dinosaur tibia.

"What do you mean, 'dinosaur bones are better than **kibble**'?" said Stewart with alarm, turning to see the dogs mouthing the T. rex.

Waldo and Sassy stopped eating the ferocious dinosaur for a moment. "If ancient dogs caught a dinosaur and brought it home, could the humans make it into a **roast**? Where did they get an oven big enough?" asked Waldo.

"There weren't dogs or humans at the same time as dinosaurs," said Stewart.

"But let's pretend there were," said Sassy. "Because I can imagine it so much, that I'm pretty sure it's true. Let's say that ancient dogs could bring this much **meat** home. It would be good, right?"

"Picture this," said Waldo. "It's dusk. The wind rustles quietly through the"—he squinted at the sign next to a big plant nearby—"prehistoric ferns. Somewhere, in the distance, you hear the distinctive roar of a giant dinosaur. Your faithful dog puts his nose in the air and sniffs! He can track the dinosaur! He's on the run! 'Be careful!' you shout as you watch your good dog race into the trees. A few moments later, your dog returns, dragging a dinosaur behind him. Hooray! Then you make the dinosaur into one million billion **hot dogs**, and everything is great."

"Where is everyone?" asked Sassy.

CHAPTER SEVEN

$\mathcal{S}$ tewart and the dogs were now alone in the dinosaur room.

"I guess everyone left while you were dreaming about catching a dinosaur," said Stewart. "Wow."

"We're lost!" said Waldo.

"We will have to stay here and keep tasting dinosaur bones," said Sassy.

"Let's walk around," said Stewart. "I bet we'll find the group."

The dogs didn't want to see any more of the museum. They didn't want to leave all those glorious dinosaur bones. They had only tasted *one* dinosaur. They had so many other dinosaurs to taste. They had days of dinosaur-tasting work ahead of them. Then Waldo thought of something.

"Oh! Sassy! What if there are even more bones in other rooms?" said Waldo. "Maybe there are tiger bones or mastodon bones or an artistic display of **steak** samples."

"You're right. We should walk around," said Sassy. "You can be the tour guide, Stewart!"

"I want to be tour guide!" said Waldo. "If I can't eat dinosaurs, I want to guide a tour."

"That actually sounds fun," said Stewart.

"But we were promised an **ice cream** party, and if they find out we're missing, we won't get **ice cream**," said Sassy.

"Yes! I want **ice cream**!" said Waldo. "And Stewart wants **ice cream**! I assume. Do you want **ice cream**, Stewart?"

"Of course I want **ice cream**," said Stewart. "And a Good Job sticker! I only need one more sticker to get that pencil, and I definitely won't get a sticker if she notices we're gone."

Sometimes, when students were very helpful, or behaved properly by not throwing desks around or chasing squirrels in the room, Ms. Twohey would give them a sticker. You could save up your stickers to buy something from the classroom store. Stewart really wanted a metallic pencil. There was only one, and he was worried about someone else getting enough stickers to get that pencil.

Salty had gotten some stickers too. The dogs could never decide what to buy with their stickers, because there was no **food** in the classroom store. So they gave all their stickers to Stewart. Except for one day, when Ms. Twohey had scratch-and-sniff stickers that smelled like **hamburgers**, and Sassy ate it before they could give it to Stewart. She felt bad, because if she hadn't eaten it, Stewart would have been able to get that shiny pencil. She also felt bad because it didn't even taste like a **hamburger**. Waldo felt bad because Sassy had gotten to eat the sticker before he even thought of it.

Waldo knew what his job was. To make sure Stewart was having fun at the museum. And if he was being a tour guide, sure, he could do that. But also his job was to be a good student. And if he abandoned the school tour, was he a bad student? What if Ms. Twohey saw him leading his own tour? Maybe she'd give him a Good Job sticker for being a good student and then take it away for being a bad student. She had never taken a sticker away before, but so many things were new today. Would she still give him **ice cream**? Surely students got separated from the group all the time. That was why they had to wear Bea Arthur **bananas**, so everyone would know at all times that they were part of the Bea Arthur Memorial Elementary School City Museum tour group. And if Ms. Twohey saw that Waldo was being an extra-good student by leading a tour, she would not be mad at him.

But Stewart smelled nervous. Waldo and Sassy could tell that Stewart was thinking about the metallic pencil again, and how he only needed one more sticker to get it. And **ice cream**. They were all thinking about **ice cream**. In order to get both, they had to find the group. They could learn about ancient bones and smell old **meat** while they were looking for the rest of the group though, right? Of course. Then they could be a good student and make Stewart happy all at the same time.

They walked out of the dinosaur room. It was true— a tour led by Waldo was going to be interesting. Stewart had been on the official tour so many times, he had it memorized. Hanging out with Waldo and Sassy in the museum instead of listening to the same fun facts and long-winded stories was going to be the best.

"Let's go this way," said Stewart.

"Hello to my tour!" said Waldo. "Sassy, tell me if you smell our human student friends. You're closer to the ground. Help me find them."

"All I smell is ancient dust and **food** somewhere in the distance," said Sassy. "And these boots."

"What boots?" said Waldo and Stewart at the same time.

"These fancy boots that are good to chew on. I found them. They're mine." Sassy stopped walking and sat down. She stuck her head out of the trench coat and dropped the rocket-powered astro-boots out of her mouth.

"Sassy!" said Waldo. "You aren't supposed to touch the art! It says so right here on the index card!"

"They are not art," said Sassy. "They are rocket boots."

"You're definitely not supposed to take the rocket boots," said Stewart.

"They are very nice to chew on," said Sassy.

"She has a point," said Waldo.

"I'm pretty sure Ms. Twohey's not going to be happy about you chewing on those boots," said Stewart.

"But they remind me of the ones I had when I was a puppy," said Sassy. "Ms. Twohey will understand that."

"Ms. Twohey doesn't even know you're the bottom half of Salty," said Stewart.

"Here you will see a hall," said Waldo as they started to walk again. "It is very large. There are no dinosaurs. Oh! Here is a room. Let's go into it. See this sign? It says *Tapestry Room*. As we all know, a tapestry is a kind of **pastry** topped with **cheese**."

"I don't think that's what a tapestry is," said Stewart.

"It really sounds like a **food**," said Waldo.

They walked into the room, where a guard leaning against the wall followed their every move. Several massive woven tapestries hung on the wall. The tapestries had designs of groups of tiny white people sitting on lawns, surrounded by horses and castles.

"These are **pastries**," said Waldo. "Or . . . tapestries. That's what they are. They are pictures of people and horses but no dogs."

"I like the idea of someone making a picture of your family, but making it into a cozy blanket," said Sassy. "Why are these on the wall? They should be on the floor. This room would be a lot easier to nap in if they put all these blankets on the floor."

"They're supposed to be like paintings, I guess," said Stewart.

"But they're not paintings. They are cozy blankets and I am tired. And hungry. And also I smell Bax."

"I can also smell Bax!" said Waldo. "BAX? BAX! WHERE ARE YOU?"

"No yelling," said the guard.

Just then the guard's walkie-talkie crackled. "We have a situation in the dinosaur room," said a voice over the walkie-talkie. "Someone has been licking the T. rex."

The guard removed her walkie-talkie from her belt and pressed a button. "Roger that. Any clues as to the perpetrator?"

"We're triangulating the parameters, but bite mark evidence so far suggests it was a small dog."

"I'm sorry, there was some interference, it sounded like you said the perpetrator is a small dog," said the guard.

"You heard right," said the voice on the walkie-talkie. "That's what I said. Small dog."

"And that's the end of our tapestry tour!" said Waldo. "Bye!"

They ran out the door into the hallway, where they found Bax.

"Oh, hey," said Bax. "I thought I heard someone calling my name, so I wandered away from the tour. I've been looking for a reason to get away from that tour all morning. It should be called a museum bore instead of a museum tour. Oh! And our tour guide should be named Boredy instead of Gordy. I'm surprised I'm still awake. What are you all doing?"

"We are having our own tour," said Waldo, "until we can get unlost and find the regular tour for **ice cream** and stickers. Do you want to come with us?"

"You bet I want to be on your tour," said Bax, taking off his bandana. "It's already been better in the past twelve seconds than the whole last forty-five minutes was following Boredy around."

CHAPTER EIGHT

Bax was intent on getting as far away from the Bea Arthur Elementary tour as possible.

"Let's go to the Renaissance paintings," said Bax. "Because Boredy's tour just came from there. So, who's leading *this* tour?"

"It is me!" said Waldo. "And don't worry, I will not talk to you like you are a puppy. I will treat you like the grown-ups you are."

"We're not grown-ups," said Bax. "But okay."

They found the Renaissance painting room. Sassy made sure they walked in a wide arc to stay as far away from the guard as possible.

"Here is a room, and it is mostly all paintings of people," said Waldo. "Some of them have wings. All of them are bored. Some of them have no clothes on and the rest are wearing too many clothes. Five skirts and four shirts each."

"It's like they're all carrying beds around with them
at all times," whispered Sassy. "For napping."

The guard walked over to stand right behind them. "Stay eighteen inches away from the artwork at all times," he said.

Just then a voice came out of his walkie-talkie. "We found a significant amount of drool on the T. rex," said the voice. "We're bringing it to the lab for analysis."

"I'll be looking for any suspects," said the guard standing behind Salty.

"Uh, maybe we should leave this room and go check out the portraits," said Stewart.

"Yes," said Waldo. "The paw prints. Lead the way."

They walked out of the Renaissance painting room and immediately ran into Ralph.

"I thought I saw you down here," said Ralph.

"You can help us find the others!" said Waldo.

"Why?" said Ralph.

"Or you can come with us on Salty's tour," said Bax.

"Technically, that's why I'm here," said Ralph.

"Stewart is wanting to have ice cream later," said Waldo. "And so am I. Also we want a Good Job sticker. Those are nice. Sometimes they smell like lunch. And I will not eat it if it does."

"Sometimes I don't know what you're talking about," said Bax.

"I am from Liver, Ohio," said Waldo. "It is important to be a good student. Won't Ms. Twohey be mad because we're not there?"

"She's not even going to notice we're gone," said Bax.

"It's true," said Ralph. "She is only paying attention to all the facts on the tour. She isn't watching the students at all."

Stewart, Bax, and Ralph followed Salty down another hallway. It took a while. They couldn't smell Ms. Twohey or any of their other friends from Bea Arthur Elementary. They could smell **food** somewhere. Should they pursue **food** now or wait for ice cream later? Which one would make Stewart happy? Could they gather all the **food** from now and the ice cream from later, make sure Stewart wasn't bored, plus get a sticker?

"Uh, hey, Salty," said Bax. "You okay?"

"Today is a lot," said Waldo. "Everything in here is so new."

"Technically, most of it is actually really old," said Ralph.

"But it is new to me," said Waldo.

Three guards ran down the hall past them.

"To the lab!" one of them shouted.

"Oh, is there a lab here?" asked Waldo.

"I wonder if it's Mozzarella," whispered Sassy. "She's a lab, right?"

ere are even more paw prints of people who do not look happy," said Waldo, looking around the portrait gallery. "Listen here, tour friends, we should be very happy we live in the now and did not travel back in time like Gordy wanted us to do. In the past, everyone had a serious and sad face all the time. Life in the past was a top-notch bummer."

Waldo walked slowly around the room, looking at the portraits, and keeping an eye on the guard by the door. The guard was watching Salty too. Most of the portraits were men. Some were women. A few were children. All were white people staring into the middle distance, with strangely pained looks on their faces.

"In the past, people liked to sit and do hobbies in the almost darkness near piles of **fruit**. They are all near the **fruit** but they never eat the **fruit**," said Waldo. "That helps explain why they were so sad."

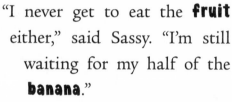

"I never get to eat the **fruit** either," said Sassy. "I'm still waiting for my half of the **banana**."

"Are you going to tell us a fun fact or a long story about the people in these portraits?" asked Ralph.

"Nope," said Waldo. "No fun facts about the paw prints."

But then suddenly Waldo spotted something in one of the paintings.

"Now here is a paw print of a happy person, finally!" said Waldo.

"He doesn't look happy," said Bax.

"But he has a dog. So of course he's happy."
The portrait was of a man wearing a velvet suit and a big floppy hat, sitting on the edge of a chair. A small dog sat attentively at his feet.

"There is a good girl over there," whispered Sassy.

"Ah, yes, and look at this one!" Waldo led the group to a painting of three young children running with a small spotted terrier. "Look at all the fun they are having! Even in olden times they recognized the importance of running and playing in the fields with your best dog. They can run around that windmill, and if they get hungry they can pick the **apples** from that tree. This might be a painting of heaven? This is an example of what is generally called Very Very Good Art and it is one of my favorite paintings in the world."

"Who painted it?" asked Bax.

"I have no idea," said Waldo. "And it does not matter. Once art has been made it belongs to all of us. So someone did paint it but now it is ours to have and love. Oh, look at that one! That is a very big dog!"

"Technically, that's a horse," said Ralph.

"Oh! There is another good one!" Waldo led the group to a smaller painting. The guard followed them, sighing dramatically. Waldo waved his arms around to point at things, like Gordy had. It was a painting of a spaniel playing the harp. The dog looked out of the painting knowingly, its long, lustrous ears ruffling gently in the breeze coming in through an open window. There was a golden music stand set up, with very complex sheet music on it.

"That sure is one talented dog," said Bax.

"All dogs are talented," said Waldo.

"Yeah, but they can't play the harp," said Ralph.

"Maybe they can," said Stewart. "Just because you've never seen one playing the harp, doesn't mean they can't."

Sassy walked in a circle. She was getting antsy. This was way too much standing and talking.

"Where are you going?" asked Bax.

"Sometimes I have to walk a bit," said Waldo, balancing. "Sometimes I have to run, even."

"Me too," said Bax. "Running is great. We're not usually allowed to run on City Museum day."

"I know," said Waldo. "It says so right here on my rule card. 'No running.' Do you think that's for the whole day? Do you think a little bit of running would be okay?"

"No running!" said the guard, who had been listening to their conversation. "Seems like a guide would know to use walking feet."

A noise came from the guard's walkie-talkie. "Alert! Alert! More vandalism! The rocket boots are missing from the space room!"

The guard pressed a button on the walkie-talkie. "Any more clues about who is doing this?"

"They found two types of fur at the scene. We think it could be two dogs instead of one."

"Ridiculous! We'd know if there were two dogs loose in the museum. Over and out."

The guard moved closer to them. "Are you supposed to be in a small group on your own?" he asked.

"Yes! We are!" said Bax. "And now we're leaving!"

They ran out of the portrait room.

CHAPTER TEN

They met five more of their classmates in the hall. "Why are you smiling?" asked Piper. "No one ever smiles on City Museum field trip day."

"We've gone rogue," said Bax. "We're doing a rebel tour. Salty's our tour guide. It's awesome."

"He doesn't talk to us like we're babies," said Stewart.

"And there are no long, boring stories," said Ralph.

"Has Ms. Twohey noticed we're gone?" asked Stewart.

"Not even a little bit," said Piper.

"**Right now we are going to find a place to run in circles and not get in trouble!**" said Waldo. "**Do you want to come on our tour?**"

"Absolutely yes," said Piper.

The atrium was a huge open room with a ceiling made of glass. Stone benches lined the perimeter, and other people were eating **snacks** or resting on the benches. Trees and plants grew from urns shaped like larger-than-life lion heads. A fountain was in the middle of the room.

"**Okay, so here is a plan,**" said Waldo. "**We are going to be like the children in that portrait, where they were running in the field. Instead of running around the windmill, we will run around that fountain. Instead of picking apples from the trees, we will not pick apples from any trees. Ready? Go!**"

Everyone started running. Gosh, it felt good to run. Or good to balance on top of a running Sassy, if you were Waldo. Or run really fast and then slide on your knees as far as you could across the slippery floor, if you were Bax. The other students had told Waldo that they were not allowed to run, but that was silly. Here was this museum, with its giant open spaces, perfect for a good run. This was not a place to walk slowly and nap when no one was

looking. What a fantastic, brilliant revelation it was, to be able to run in this giant room. Where else would they be able to run? In the long, wide hallways? Outside? Back to the dinosaur room, where all those giant bones were waiting?

"No running!" yelled a guard.

"We are not running," said Waldo. "We are experiencing art."

"What's that now?" said the guard. "Don't try to

pull the grass over my eyes. I saw you just now, running."

"We are learning what it's like to be in a painting," said Waldo.

"You know," said Ralph, catching his breath, "*Gallivanting Children and Dog* by Rosa Artiste. It's in the portrait room."

"Oh," said the guard. "Well, carry on, then."

The dogs were thirsty, and there, right in front of them, was a giant dish of water. Sure, there was a narwhal statue in the middle of it, and water was shooting out of the narwhal's eye sockets, but it was an enormous amount of water. No one would notice if some water was missing.

Waldo looked around to see if anyone would notice if he stuck his face in the fountain. Then he decided he didn't care. He was thirsty.

Sassy was thirsty too. She had been the one doing all that running, after all.

"I wish the water bowl at home was this big," said Sassy.

Sassy realized the best way for both of them to drink would be for her to stand in the fountain. So she did. Sassy leaned in and slurped at the water, and

Waldo did his best to drink from the water shooting out of the narwhal.

It was refreshing, and messy.

Sassy stepped out of the fountain and shook off the water. Waldo shook off the water too.

"Hey, how do you do that?" asked Piper. "I don't know if I can dance like that."

"Yeah, that's pretty cool," said Bax. "What's that move called?"

"It is called the I'm Hungry," said Waldo. "I am from Liver, Ohio."

"Uh, we should get going," said Stewart. "Those guards over there look like they suspect something."

"I didn't do anything," said Bax. "Not today."

"I want to learn how to do the I'm Hungry," said Piper.

Waldo stood in front of the students and shook off the remaining water droplets. Sassy shook a bit too, although more timidly. She was nervous about it now that everyone thought she was dancing. The students did their best to shake like Salty was doing, but it wasn't easy (probably because they had only two arms and two legs).

A group of three guards on the opposite side of the atrium were pointing at Salty and talking into their walkie-talkies, and started walking purposefully toward them.

"No unauthorized tour may be given by the fountain!" shouted a guard.

"And have any of you seen any naughty dogs running amok?" shouted another.

"**Biscuits,** let's get out of here!" shouted Waldo, and they ran out of the atrium.

CHAPTER ELEVEN

L et's get to a place where we can give authorized tours!" said Waldo.

They followed Salty down one hallway, up another, up an elevator, and down another wide hall. They were all so exhilarated by running from the guards that they weren't even paying attention to where they were going. Also, because they weren't paying attention, no one noticed that they had acquired several more Bea Arthur Elementary students until they all stopped, panting, and waited for Salty to figure out where to go next.

"Oh, look, the dioramas," said Stewart. "We should go in there. You'll love those, Salty."

"A diorama is a rotating display of **desserts**, right?" said Waldo.

"If there are **desserts** spinning in circles, you need to knock some off into my mouth," said Sassy. "Also where are all those **lunches** I was promised? I need all my **lunches** before I eat all these **desserts**."

"Uh, no," said Stewart. "It's a little scene set up to show what prehistoric life or animal habitats were like."

"I wish it was a rotating display of **desserts**," said Waldo.

"You and me both," said Bax.

They heard footsteps around the corner.

"Can you believe the space room guard really thinks there could be two dogs running around in here?" said one guard to another.

"I believe it," said the other guard. "Rusty from portraits said there was more than one dog's worth of drool in the sample."

"**Dioramas it is!**" said Waldo, running into the diorama wing before the guards came around the corner, even though it had nothing to do with **dessert**. Or any **food**.

There was another guard in this room, and he eyed the group warily. Sassy walked in a big arc around the guard, giving him lots of space.

"**We are a good tour group!**" said Waldo. "**We will not use any flashlights! We love guards! Guards are the best!**"

"Tour guides, ugh," the guard groaned under his breath.

The first room was all African animals. Waldo and Sassy had never seen anything like it. A herd of elephants stood on a platform in the center of the room, trunks raised, eyes fixed on the entrance to the exhibit and, it seemed, on Waldo and Sassy. Sassy stopped walking. Waldo stood on her back, motionless.

"Everybody shhh," said Waldo. "The slightest movement will cause these elephants to jump down and trample us all."

"No, it's—" said Stewart.

"There are lions!" said Waldo. "Lions! Over there! And they are eating a zebra! That is good. They will not be hungry after they eat that zebra. Unless they might want to eat us as an after-zebra **snack**?"

"What kind of museum is this?" whispered Sassy. "Isn't it careless to put wild animals in a room and then send tour groups of delectable children into the room to be trampled and eaten?"

"You know what is weird though?" Waldo whispered back. "None of these fearsome beasts are moving."

"Do you think," said Sassy, "it's because we're so fierce?"

"These are wild animals," Waldo announced, leading the tour again. "It is important they know we're very fierce. We need to be the alpha beasties, so they know we'll win in a fight."

"I don't want to fight," said Piper.

"Neither do I," said Waldo. "These elephants look tusky."

Stewart cleared his throat. "So, uh, these are dioramas, like I was telling you. Taxidermied animals in scenes to show what they're like in the wild."

"Does taxidermied mean stunned by my ferocity?" asked Waldo.

"It means they don't move," said Bax. "They're stuffed."

"Technically, it's a bit more complicated than that," said Ralph.

"But they don't move," said Becky.

"WELL, THAT IS A HUGE RELIEF," said Waldo. "Okay, let's start the tour, then. Wait, you're sure they're not going to move?"

Everyone nodded.

The guard's walkie-talkie crackled. "Lab tests confirm: DNA of two dogs present in several exhibit rooms."

"Oh, there is a door that we can go through into another room. Which is a relief," said Waldo.

The new room was called *Wild/Domestic* and featured dioramas of wild animals who lived in cities and suburbs, near people. There was a deer munching on flowers in someone's garden. There were birds around a bird feeder and in a birdbath. Some wild turkeys were looking for **food** on the side of a road. A raccoon had overturned a garbage can and was grabbing a **chicken bone**.

And then Waldo and Sassy saw it. It was like a dream. It was, in fact, something they had both dreamed about many times. It was always the best dream. But this was no dream. It was real. Squirrels peeking out of every tree hole, from behind every leaf high on a branch. Squirrels in the gutter of a house and under a bush by the walkway. A squirrel on the sidewalk, shoving an acorn into its mouth. So many squirrels.

"Squirreltown," said Waldo.

"It's so beautiful, I can hardly look at it," said Sassy.

Waldo realized he was audibly panting. The others were staring. Or maybe they were staring at the squirrels. He sure found the squirrel diorama to be riveting. But he knew his job. His job was to get rid of squirrels. Oh, also it was to be a top-notch tour guide.

"Okay! Tour humans!" said Waldo. "Right here is a diorama of something I know a lot about. It is called Squirreltown. Did you know that Squirreltown is a place where all the squirrels will go someday? One day you will go outside Bea Arthur Memorial Elementary and there will be no squirrels, and do you know why?"

"Uh, Squirreltown?" asked Becky.

"Exactly. Squirreltown," said Waldo. "All the squirrels will be in Squirreltown, setting up their own town councils and television networks, and all the dogs will finally nap."

"Technically," said Ralph, reading the plaque on the wall, "this is just a diorama of squirrels. It doesn't say anything about Squirreltown."

"But that is what it is," said Waldo. "I know about these things. You are very lucky to get a glimpse of Squirreltown. Not everyone is so lucky."

Sassy had moved closer and closer to the squirrel diorama, and now she whispered something up to Waldo.

"Yes," said Waldo dreamily. "Yes."

"What are you saying yes to?" asked Stewart suspiciously.

Waldo leaned over and whispered to Stewart. "It is our job to get rid of all the squirrels. All of them. And wouldn't it be nice to hold a squirrel in your mouth? Doesn't that sound fun?"

"No," said Stewart. "And it doesn't sound fun to you either." He looked down to about where Sassy was under the trench coat. "Or to you."

"I really think it's important for us to get inside that diorama of Squirreltown," said Waldo.

Just then three guards came into the *Wild/Domestic* exhibit.

"We're going to have to search this room," one guard said. "There was a pile of dog hair back near the elephants plus a chewed-up piece of a rocket boot."

"Hey!" said another guard to Salty. "You haven't seen any dogs around, have you?"

"No!" said Waldo. "I **have not!**"

"Tour guides don't pay attention to things like dogs running loose," said one of the guards to the others. "They're too focused on being boring."

"That's not very nice," said Waldo.

"Hey, did you see another tour walking around?" asked Bax. "Boring guy talking to an enthusiastic teacher lady, with a dwindling group of students? We're trying to avoid them."

"That describes every tour," said a guard.

"Yeah, but did you see them?" asked Stewart. "Maybe it's time we headed back."

"We've really been focused on this criminal case," said a guard. "We haven't been paying attention to any of the tours. Here's what we're looking for. Two dogs, who drool, at least in the presence of dinosaurs. These dogs shed. And are likely in possession of some rocket boots."

"Are the rocket boots priceless artifacts?" asked Waldo.

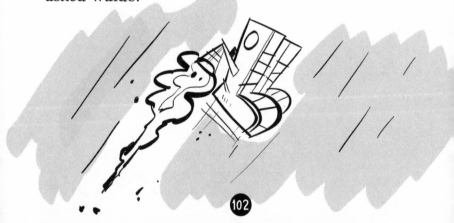

"No, they're actually not worth much at all," said a guard. "But that's not the point. Dogs are running loose somewhere in this museum and we can't find them. Anyway, remember that list: two dogs, drooling, lots of hair, rocket boots. Write it down."

"I really wish I had that metallic pencil," said Stewart. "It'd be perfect for writing down a list like that."

"You will get that pencil, Stewart," said Waldo. He turned toward the guards. "Now when are the visiting hours for Squirreltown? We would like the up-close-and-personal squirrel experience."

"No one's getting close to any squirrels until we find the dogs who licked a dinosaur," said a guard.

"And stole the space boots!" said another.

"And sprayed water droplets all over the fountain area of the atrium," said the third.

"There are no dogs in the dioramas," said the first guard into his walkie-talkie, while scanning the displays with an infrared heat tracker. "It was a smart guess that the loose dogs would find their way to these squirrels, but they're not here." The guards all ran out of the room.

"They are running away!" said Waldo. "Because they did not find any dogs! Which is good news! Now is our chance to visit Squirreltown!" He and Sassy started to look for a door into the squirrel display.

"The most important thing is for us to get out of here as fast as we can," said Stewart.

CHAPTER TWELVE

I am worried we won't get **ice cream** or Good Job stickers." Waldo yawned. "Also I need to nap. Also I am very hungry. I ate my first **lunch** for second **breakfast** and my second **lunch** for first **lunch** and I had **carrots** in my backpack but I think I spilled them all somewhere because they're all gone."

"I put them in the rocket boots and ate them," said Sassy. "Turns out space boots are the perfect **snack** dispenser. Also I was promised so many **lunches**. And all I've gotten are boot **carrots**."

All dogs are able to smell how the humans near them are feeling. Waldo and Sassy could tell that Arden felt confident, Ralph felt superior, Becky was internally laughing at a joke her brother had told her at **breakfast**, and Stewart was worried about someone else buying that shiny pencil from the classroom store.

"We need to find MS. Twohey so we get **ice cream** and a sticker. Don't you think she's looking for us?" asked Waldo.

"No," said Arden. "Last I saw her, she and Gordy were talking about how to make a pen out of an emu feather. She wasn't paying attention to us at all."

"Do you think she knows we're all lost?"

Arden looked around. "We're not lost."

"But where is lunch?" asked Waldo. "How can we have lunch right now if Ms. Twohey doesn't know where we are?"

"Also, technically, we're not allowed to eat in here," said Ralph.

Just then a big group of guards rushed toward them.

"Down to the lab in the west wing," shouted a guard. "We've got the results of the fingerprinting!"

"Paw printing, you mean?" said another guard.

"Dogs have funny little hands, don't they?" said another.

Waldo looked surreptitiously at his own paws. "Hands that are strong and confident and good at rooting out cheese shreds from under the refrigerator."

"Yes, thank you for that, mine are too big," said Sassy.

"Come on! Let's go! We have to hurry and find out what the results say!" said the guard. "Hopefully they have a positive ID on who the drooling, messy, shedding boot thief is!"

Stewart and Waldo made eye contact once the guards were past. The guards were looking for them. It was a good thing no one had noticed the rocket boots that Sassy had shoved into an internal pocket of the trench coat so she could casually chew on them or eat **carrots** out of them while she walked.

"Phew, that was close," said Waldo.

"What do you mean?" asked Arden.

"It was physically close," said Stewart. "Those guards brushed right past us."

"I am starving so much," whispered Sassy. "You are up there getting rotating displays of **desserts** and five or twelve or nine hundred **lunches** in convenient bags so you can eat them whole, and I am eating *boots* down here. *Boots.* Sure, they're extremely satisfying to chew on, but they are not **lunch**. That's one of the dog mottos, right? Boots Are Not **Lunch**, Unless They're Full of **Sandwiches**, and guess what? They are not full of **sandwiches**."

"They were full of **carrots** before," said Waldo.

"But they are not full of **carrots** now, and carrots are not **sandwiches**," said Sassy, harrumphing.

"So," said Waldo to everyone, "I believe we were talking about **lunch**."

"I'm hungry too," said Bax.

"It's probably time for us to head to the delicatessen," said Ralph.

"Oh, what's the delicatessen?" asked Waldo. "Is it a craft room for children? Is it portraits of a king? An interactive display about hedgehogs?"

"No, it's the place where they make **sandwiches**," said Ralph.

"Really?" said Waldo. "You are not joking with me? It's a **sandwich** place?"

"It's really **sandwiches**," said Stewart.

"What are we waiting for?" asked Waldo. "To the delicatessen we go!"

The delicatessen was downstairs, on the main floor. The students waited outside the elevator. Waldo pressed the elevator button repeatedly. The doors slid open with a ding, and they all got in.

"Is this a robot delicatessen?" asked Waldo.

"This is an elevator," said Stewart.

"Ah," said Waldo. "I see."

Nothing happened. Waldo was waiting for his **sandwich**. If he couldn't get a delicatessen **sandwich**, he would settle for an elevator **sandwich**.

"It doesn't seem like there's any **food** in here," Waldo said finally.

"There's no **food** in here either," grumbled Sassy from inside the coat.

"There's not," said Ralph.

"Why are we here?" asked Waldo. "Is it to listen to this song? Is this a radio cube?"

"This is just regular old elevator music," said Arden. "It's all the same."

"Technically, that's not true," said Ralph. "Elevator music is a specific type of relaxing instrumental music derived from popular songs. For instance, this is a version of the 'Cha Cha Slide,' which I danced to with my bubbe at my cousin's bar mitzvah."

"But it does not result in a **sandwich**?" asked Waldo.

"No," said Stewart.

The elevator stopped moving, and the doors opened, and then the dogs could smell it. The **food**.

CHAPTER THIRTEEN

Sassy practically skipped down the hall, while Waldo sang, "Delicatessen! Delicatessen!"

When they got to the **food** court, they were stunned. It was more than just a delicatessen. It was a huge room, like the cafeteria back at Bea Arthur Memorial Elementary, but with **food** counters around the edges of the room. The dogs could smell so many different kinds of **food**, coming from every direction.

"I- Hey. This is more than just a delicatessen," said Waldo. "Oh! I know what I have to do! This part I can do!"

The tour group, which somehow had grown even larger since they left the dioramas, looked bewildered.

"Do not worry!" said Waldo. "I will tour you through all the delicatessens! Follow me!"

The students walked after Salty, who bounded up to the first **food** counter.

"Fun fact: **Sandwiches** need to have two pieces of **bread**! **Sandwiches** were invented by someone with too much **bread** who wanted to eat **lunch** while also riding a donkey! If someone tells you they made a **sandwich** but with two pieces of **chicken** instead of **bread**, tell them that it's not a **sandwich**, and then steal the thing they made and bring it to me!"

"We only have **pizza** here," said the man behind the counter.

"This is **pizza**!" said Waldo. "**Pizza** is not a **sandwich**. But it is very delicious. Fun fact: You should always get the **pizza** called Supreme or Deluxe or, in the best possible scenario, **Supreme Deluxe**. That has all the **meat**."

"Is that what you want?" said the man behind the counter, getting a paper plate.

"Okay, yes!" said Waldo.

"I was promised one dozen **lunches**," said Sassy with conviction as she walked down to the next counter, which was a **salad** bar.

"This is like a make-your-own-art exhibit," said Waldo to the students. "You assemble your own **food** here, in an artful way. It's for if you want to be an artist and also you are hungry. These hard rocks can be used to support the food sculpture you create."

"Technically, those are **croutons**," said Ralph.

"These mini cubes of **ham** were used by medieval kings when they were playing card games with their friends," said Waldo. "That is how dice were invented." He reached his paw toward the bin of **ham** cubes.

"Use the tongs!" yelled a server on the other side of the counter.

"Why?" asked Waldo.

"You're not going to make a **salad** anyway, are you?" said Stewart.

"I **can and I will!**" said Waldo, using the tongs to pile **ham** cubes and **shredded cheese** into a bowl.

"Hey, you are being too neat!" whispered Sassy.

Waldo grabbed more **ham** and **cheese**, but dropped most of it on the floor.

"Thank you," said Sassy.

"Why are we even here?" said a girl. "I have my **lunch** in my backpack. Don't you? We should go sit at those tables and eat."

"I accidentally ate my **lunch** for **snack** and my **snack** for **snack** while everyone was looking at outer space," said Waldo.

"Do you go to Bea Arthur Elementary?" Stewart asked the girl.

"No, I go to Phyllis Diller Prep. I saw your tour and it looked better than the same boring tour we go on every year." The girl looked around. "Half of these people are from my school."

"That is good news! Our tour wins! I hope that means we still get **ice cream** and that Stewart will get a sticker. You can eat your backpack **lunch** or you can give it to me," said Waldo. "Or you can eat it and get more **food** right now. Also you can get drinks, I hope, or I will have to go back to the fountain."

"Now? The fountain is way back in the atrium," said Piper.

"No, that is a human expression that means I am thirsty," said Waldo. "Also I am hungry. Wait, what is that counter over there?"

"Hi!" said the smiling lady on the other side of the counter. "This is the **beef** bowl station. Do you want a **beef** bowl for **lunch**?"

"I have never wanted anything more in my entire life," said Waldo, who was drooling slightly.

"What size do you want?" asked the lady.

"The largest possible size," said Waldo.

"Get two!" said Sassy.

"Do you want **pork** on your **beef**?" asked the lady.

"Yes, please!" said Waldo.

"Extra **bacon**!" said Sassy.

"Do you want **cheese** sauce on your **beef** bowl?"

Waldo had to lean against the sneeze guard to steady himself. It was too much. He was feeling faint. "Yes, **cheese**," he said.

"That'll be twenty-four dollars," said the lady, handing a steaming bowl of **cheesy meat** over to Waldo.

"Oh!" said Waldo.

"Yeah, I know," said the lady conspiratorially. "The prices in here are outrageous."

Waldo didn't have any money. He had never in his life had any money. He raised his eyebrows. He made his eyes extra big and sad. He had trouble making sad eyes at the **beef** bowl lady because he also very much wanted to lean over and eat the entire **beef** bowl.

"Are you here on a school trip?" asked the lady.

"Yes."

"You can charge it to the trip fund," she said, taking out an official-looking notebook. "What's the name of your school?"

"Oh!" said Waldo happily. "It is **Beef** Arthur school. I mean. Bea Arthur. I'm sorry. I am very hungry."

"That's okay, champ," said the lady. "You're all set. I wrote you down for all the **food** you've got there."

"Good news, everyone!" said Waldo. "You can get all the **food** you want and tell them you're from Bea Arthur!"

Everyone scattered to various **lunch** counters while Waldo very carefully carried his extra-large **beef** bowl, pile of **ham** cubes and **shredded cheese**, and **Supreme Deluxe pizza** to a quiet corner behind a plant, where he dumped it onto the floor so both he and Sassy could eat it. Though he did leave some of it in the bowl. And he ate that. That was only fair, for having to do all that important ordering and figuring out and **cheese sauce** getting. Plus for being the tour guide.

He also ate the bowl.

Waldo noticed that his index cards of rules had accidentally fallen on the floor. He happened to see one that said, "Do Not Charge Items to the School Account Without Teacher Permission."

"Oops. Well," said Waldo to himself, casually eating that index card, "too bad that rule doesn't exist anymore. And if only Ms. Twohey hadn't gotten lost, I'm sure she would have given us permission."

"I am very thirsty," said Sassy. "I have never been this thirsty in my life. I am the world's thirstiest dog. I cannot make it one more second unless I have something to drink."

Waldo found the juice box that had been in their bag lunch at the bottom of his backpack.

"I will save the day," Waldo whispered back to Sassy. "We will have something called Tropical Fun in the Sun Flavor Juice-Type Product."

"'Tropical fun in the sun' sounds like it will make me even thirstier," said Sassy.

"It is implying that we will drink it and feel refreshed," said Waldo.

Waldo put the juice box on the floor. Sassy tried to drink through the straw, but she couldn't get any out. She leaned over to get a better grip on the juice box, thinking that might be the problem, and squirted all the juice out of the box and onto the floor. She licked it up quickly. It tasted like someone's idea of a **pineapple** and also like museum dirt.

Then they napped for a bit while all the other students ate their **lunches**. It was a lot of students. Waldo wondered if they would ever find Ms. Twohey again. It was a funny feeling to be so lost, but at least he was lost with all his friends. If they never found Ms. Twohey, they would have to live in the City Museum. He'd have to pull down one of those antique tapestries to sleep on, probably. He'd have to swim in the fountain, probably. He'd have to eat a dinosaur, definitely.

"Listen, Sassy," said Waldo, "I know we want to eat more dinosaurs, but we probably won't get a Good Job sticker for eating a triceratops."

"That's true," said Sassy. "Someone else might get a sticker. Someone else who doesn't eat a dinosaur. And then they might get Stewart's pencil. Also I want **ice cream**. I never get **ice cream**. You have maybe been eating **ice cream** all day up there, and I don't even know. Give me **ice cream**."

"You know what we have to do," said Waldo.

"Find Ms. Twohey, get the sticker, have the **ice cream**," said Sassy. "Should we get another **beef** bowl first?"

"Absolutely yes."

CHAPTER FOURTEEN

All right. Okay. Let's get moving, again!" Waldo was looking at a large and eager group of elementary school students. Word had spread. Everyone knew that there was a new tour at the museum, and it was much more entertaining than the regular tour. The tour guide didn't drone on for hours. The fun facts were more fun than they were facts. The only way to make it through a City Museum tour was to join up with Salty's group.

Waldo was having a good time, except for the part about worrying about Stewart not getting a Good Job sticker. Stewart really wanted that pencil. Sometimes at night, as they drifted off to sleep, Stewart would talk about all his favorite office supplies, and how great that pencil would look with them. Sassy said she thought the best part about pencils was when you chewed them up to see what was inside, but Stewart said he wanted to write with the pencil.

Maybe Stewart would get a Good Job sticker for being such a good student on the field trip. But maybe also Salty would get a Good Job sticker, and then the dogs could give it to Stewart, and he could get the pencil because they helped. And that would make up for the time Sassy ate the scratch-and-sniff sticker that smelled like delicious **hamburgers**.

Waldo was learning one million things on this field trip. He was being a good student, good enough for a sticker. He puffed up a bit. Ms. Twohey was going to be proud of him. Wherever she was. He hoped he'd see her again someday.

They headed into another room, where Bax had found a dress-up area, and everyone put on tricornered hats, breeches, and vests, and dueled with wooden swords.

"This room has lots of pewter cups from old-timey America," said Waldo. "Also this bed, which does not look very comfortable. This is Paul Revere. He wrote a play about cows. This is John Adams. He invented skyscrapers. This is Martha Washington. She was in an award-winning rock-and-roll band. This is Paul Revere's horse. He is actually more famous than Paul Revere. Obviously."

"Technically, you got their names right but that's it," said Ralph.

"The **bread** coats are coming! The **bread** coats are coming!" shouted Bax.

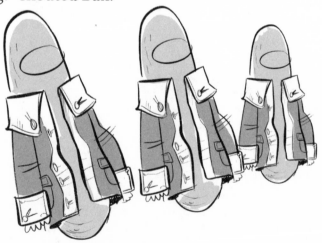

"Technically, also wrong," said Ralph.

"I'd like a coat full of **bread**," said Sassy. "Why aren't there pockets full of **bread** for me in this trench coat?"

Waldo was glad to see everyone having such a good time, but the more time went on, the more he worried about Ms. Twohey. She was not doing all the fun things they were. She was not having bowls of **beef** or **Supreme Deluxe pizza slices**. She was not visiting Squirreltown or drinking from a fountain. She was on Gordy's tour. Waldo had only been on half an hour of Gordy's tour, and that had been enough. Was it fair that they were all having so much fun and Ms. Twohey was not with them? Shouldn't she be allowed to have fun too? Poor Ms. Twohey. She would be so sad and lonely without all of them.

Meanwhile, everyone was done with dressing up as colonial Americans (it was hot, wearing woolen breeches over your regular pants) and were now on to the *American Artifacts* exhibit in the next room, and Waldo was at the helm as tour guide again.

"Here is a chair," said Waldo. "It is the world's most comfortable chair, and that's why it's in a museum."

"Actually," said Ralph, "that is Barney Cruncher's famous chair, from the *Barney Cruncher Show*."

"Has anyone ever even seen that show?" asked Becky.

"My parents watched it," said Piper. "I think."

"Here is a famous hat," said Waldo. "It has spiky feathers to confuse the predators. This is a pair of extremely sparkly shoes that are obviously magic. Here is a pair of gloves. Okay. Here are some adorable puppets, and there is a bathing suit and WHAT IS THAT?"

Sassy had seen it first, and had nipped at Waldo's toe to get him to notice it.

The dogs walked reverently toward a dog bowl. Could it be? Was it really? Yes.

"Oh," said Waldo. "Oh gosh. This is the dog bowl that belonged to Sergeant Barkles. A true hero. Sergeant Barkles carried secret messages during the war, and dragged a soldier three hundred miles to safety after the soldier had eaten some bad lettuce. Sergeant Barkles saved so many lives, plus was such a good girl. She was also, of course, the star of such amazing movies like 'A Medal for All Good Dogs' and 'Glory and Kibbles.'"

Ralph was reading the sign on the wall the whole time Waldo was talking. "That's all totally true, Salty."

"Of course it is," said Waldo. "Do you think I am making up everything on this tour?"

"Well, yes," said Ralph.

"Maybe only a little," said Waldo. "Or most of it."

An astonishingly large group of guards came running by. "Have you seen two dogs?" one of them asked. "They have been stealing boots, licking dinosaur bones, and spilling juice in the **food** court. Or it may be, and this is conjecture based on recent samples, one dog riding on the back of another dog."

"That is a real laugh and a half!" said Waldo. "We cannot help you! Goodbye!"

CHAPTER FIFTEEN

A re you worried about the guards looking for two dogs stacked up on top of each other?" whispered Stewart.

"I would be much more worried about that if I wasn't so flabbergasted about all the Sergeant Barkles stuff in this museum," said Waldo. "You never told me that." Waldo and Sassy took one last look at Sergeant Barkles's food bowl, collar, and medals, and started leading the tour to the next exhibit.

"Honestly, I forgot," said Stewart. "By the time the regular tour gets to this room, the guides have talked so much about outer space and the tapestries that we have to move pretty quickly. They never talk about Sergeant Barkles."

"That's ridiculous and an outrage," said Waldo.

"How do you know so much about Sergeant Barkles?" asked Becky as they went down the hall.

"She is one of the heroes of canine cinema!" said Waldo.

"Yeah, we've watched all her movies," said Stewart.

"You and Salty have?" said Becky. "Didn't Salty just move here? And you have already watched a bunch of old dog movies together?"

"It's 'Sergeant Barkles,'" said Waldo. "An icon. You should watch her movies too! Especially The Hero with Fleas.'"

"Okay, sure," said Becky.

Waldo looked at the room where they had stopped. "Where are we?"

"These are statues," said Stewart.

Waldo walked around, looking at the people made out of cool, creamy marble or dark bronze and granite. He wondered what the people had done to be turned to stone like that. They must have been robbers or litterers or people who didn't like dogs. And some of them had had their arms broken off! A few were missing heads! When were all the terrible people in town brought to this one room in the City Museum and put under a spell that turned them into rock people?

"This is so sad," said Waldo. "And it is a good reminder to all of us to be the best we can be. Because if you do not do your job, and don't do what you're told, you will be turned to stone!"

"These weren't people," said Arden.

"Sure they were," said Waldo. "It says right here, 'Zeus, sky god.' So that's a real person. A sky god person, who did something wrong, and was turned to stone. I wonder what he did."

"Stole someone's **breakfast**, maybe," said Bax.

"Or worse," said Waldo. "Maybe he stole two **breakfasts**."

"One of those **breakfasts** should have been mine," said Sassy.

Waldo continued to walk around the room, showing everyone how terribly sad it was that so many people had been so bad to be turned into stone. Even some babies. Even some people who didn't have clothes on. Though he couldn't figure out why, if you were told to come to the City Museum to be punished for stealing all those **breakfasts**, you would decide to show up without clothes on. Sometimes people were so confusing.

"Oh, look!" whispered Waldo to Stewart, pointing at a statue of the ancient Greek philosopher Socrates while the other classmates roamed around the statue room. "It's Socks and Rascal!"

"What, that statue of Socrates?" said Stewart.

"Socrates was their human name. But look, you can see, it's Socks and Rascal," said Waldo. "They are famous dogs. They liked to have arguments with people. They always said it was fun to win arguments. They got **cheese** when they won. See? Socks, the schnauzer, is the head, and Rascal is the feet."

"Oh, wow," said Stewart, looking closely at the statue. "I can't believe I never noticed that before. Socrates was two dogs in a toga?"

"Yes," said Waldo.

"Two dogs who would argue with people?" asked Stewart.

"Yes. They are famous for it. The Dogmatic Method," said Waldo.

"I thought it was called the Socratic Method," said Stewart.

"Either," said Waldo. "Dogmatic because they were dogs, or Socratic after Socks and Rascal. They would argue with humans. A human would say, '**Bread** is the best **food**' and then Socks would say, 'Or is it?' and finally they would decide **cheese** is better than **bread** and Socks and Rascal would get **cheese** because they won."

"How many years have we been coming to this museum, and I never noticed the dogs in that sculpture," said Stewart.

"Do not be sad about that," said Waldo. "They were experts at humaning, just like we are."

"You are pretty good at it," said Stewart. "I was worried about not getting a sticker today, but I don't know if I care anymore."

"But if you don't get a sticker, you can't get the nice pencil," said Waldo.

"Well, not today," said Stewart.

"What do you mean?"

"I could do something good and get a sticker tomorrow," said Stewart. "And then get the pencil tomorrow."

"Tomorrow?" said Sassy. "You can plan further than fifteen minutes in the future?"

"I mean, I'd really like to get the pencil as soon as possible," said Stewart. "But it's okay if I don't. Your tour is so much more fun than Gordy's."

"What's that about Gordy?" said a guard who had been hiding behind a statue of Tobias Jefferton. "He's one of those guides who is always snitching on the guard squads."

"What is a guard squad?" asked Waldo.

"It's when all the guards get together and have to leave our posts so we can nab scofflaws who drool on the dinosaur bones."

"Oh, I'm sure no one drools on the dinosaur bones!" said Waldo, trying to laugh casually, and whining instead. "That is silly!"

"It might be silly, kid, but it happens." The guard leaned in conspiratorially. "It's happening right now. You keep your eye out for two dogs, one riding the other, drooling prodigiously, and spilling juice."

"One riding the other?" said Stewart.

"That's right," said the guard. "We have a report of a half gallon of missing **ham** cubes from the **salad** bar. There's no way one dog could get up that high on their own. But two dogs acting as a team, well, they could accomplish anything, like stealing **ham** cubes."

"And **cheese!**" said Waldo.

"Oh, right, I forgot about the **cheese**," said the guard.

"Don't forget the **cheese!**" said Waldo.

"Just keep an eye out for those dogs," said the guard as he turned away. He looked up at the statue in front of him. "Socrates—one of my favorites in the museum. He was quite a man."

"I think I hear our teacher calling us!" said Stewart. "We should go!"

CHAPTER SIXTEEN

The students all ran out of the statue room, following Stewart.

"I don't hear Ms. Twohey," said Bax.

"She wasn't really calling us," said Stewart. "But we had to go."

Stewart pulled Salty to a corner.

"Did you really steal **cheese** and **ham** cubes?"

"I **did not steal them, I took them**," said Waldo. "**For my mouth.**"

"For our mouths," said Sassy.

"Do you have food?" said Bax. "I'm hungry again."

"You know what I want?" said Waldo. "Awesome nut ice cream."

"We all want ice cream," said Bax. "All the time."

"Do you mean astronaut ice cream?" asked Stewart.

"I just said that," said Waldo.

"I want to go back to the dinosaurs," said Sassy, panting under the trench coat.

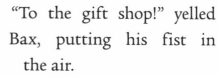

"To the gift shop!" yelled Bax, putting his fist in the air.

"The gift shop!" repeated the now impossibly large crowd of children following Salty.

The gift shop was not what Waldo and Sassy expected. It didn't make any sense. What kind of exhibit was this? It was a colorful and jumbled array of everything from minerals to stuffed animals. There were puzzles. There were note cards. There were posters and books and tiny crystal turtles.

And the students were touching *everything*.

Kids were hugging stuffed animal mastodons. Kids were trying out the pencils and markers, and flipping over the special pens where a picture of Benjamin Franklin raised a kite in the air when you turned the pen upside down. Kids were rummaging through the rocks and trying on T-shirts.

"Hello! Students! You have forgotten everything!" shouted Waldo, waving his index cards of rules. "No touching! No running! No squeezing fuzzy dinosaurs!"

"It's okay," said Stewart. "We're allowed to in here. This is the gift shop."

Gift shop. Those were two words that meant nothing to Waldo and Sassy. Why could they touch all the things in this strange exhibit called the gift shop, but not in the statue room? It was all so confusing. Especially since Waldo had gone to all the trouble of writing all the rules down on index cards. He didn't remember Ms. Twohey saying anything about how the rules applied everywhere except for in the gift shop that seemed to be a jumble of all the other exhibits, and where you were allowed to try on T-shirts that had glow-in-the-dark dinosaurs on them.

Waldo and Sassy ignored the chaos around them. They had come into the gift shop for one thing.

"Hello," said Waldo as they walked up to the counter where the cash register was. "I am looking for space people **ice cream**."

"It's right over there on the wall," said the woman behind the counter. "I like your bandana."

"It shows that I'm with my class!" said Waldo. "And also makes me look jaunty!"

"Where's your teacher?" asked the woman.

"Have you seen her?" asked Waldo.

"What?" said the woman.

"I'm going to get space **ice cream**! Because honestly we're probably not going to get an **ice cream** party at this point! Because who even knows where Ms. Twohey is! I'm from Liver, Ohio!" said Waldo as he and Sassy wandered away.

The dogs found the astronaut **ice cream**, which came in a flat, silvery pouch. They argued about which flavor to get. **Vanilla Shooting Star** sounded good, but **Minty Drifting in the Cosmos** was also tempting. They finally decided on **Supernova Strawberry**. They slid the pouch off the hook on the wall and sat on the floor, ready to eat **ice cream** like astronauts do.

Waldo ripped open the silver packet and sniffed curiously at the dry, chalky, pink block inside. He slid the cube of **ice cream** out and broke it in two, passing the smaller piece to Sassy. Shards of space **ice cream** broke onto the floor, which was odd. This was not the way **ice cream** behaved. At least not earth **ice cream**.

Both dogs shoved the astronaut **ice cream** into their mouths. It was like eating a vaguely-**strawberry**-adjacent foam block that disintegrated into gummy dust within seconds.

"How do you like the astronaut **ice cream**?" asked Stewart, finding his dogs on the floor behind the minerals.

"**It was disgusting and I also really want more,**" said Waldo. "**Because I want to be an astronaut. Who eats ice cream.**"

"Can you help me scrape the residue off my tongue?" said Sassy. "Then I want more too."

The dogs stood up and wondered about eating more astronaut **ice cream**, but also wondered if it was supposed to be eaten at all. Maybe it was like the wooden **fruit** and **cheese** that lived in a bowl at Stewart's grandma's house. Sassy had learned the hard way that the wooden **cheese** was not **cheese** and also apparently was not for chewing or putting in your mouth at all. Maybe the astronaut **ice cream** was also decorative **food**.

And then, suddenly, they saw it. A squirrel.

There it was. Right in plain sight. In a pile of stuffed animals: a tiger, an elephant, a lion, a zebra—a squirrel. Its fur was perfect and clean, and its tail was long and fluffy. It lay still in the stuffed animal bin, but the look of panic in its eyes was unmistakable.

Sassy started to whine.

"Wow, you *are* hungry," said Becky. "I can hear your stomach from here."

"It is the squirrel," said Waldo. "It must have escaped from the Squireltown exhibit."

"Oh, that squirrel there? You do talk about squirrels a lot," said Becky.

To Waldo and Sassy's absolute delight and unfettered horror, Becky stuck her hand in the stuffed animal bin and patted the squirrel on the head. She pulled the squirrel onto her lap and hugged it.

"I think you should get it," she said, waving it around a little. "It's really cute."

She gave the squirrel another squeeze. Waldo and Sassy could barely breathe.

"Here," said Becky, and then she did a remarkable thing. She threw the squirrel to Salty.

Easy as **pie**, like no big deal, there was Becky, tossing a squirrel, throwing it to Salty like it was something she did every day.

Waldo let out a little scream and lunged for the squirrel but missed. The toy squirrel rolled underneath a display case and out the door. Waldo screamed again, this one coming out as a full bark, and fell forward off Sassy into the hallway, who ran toward the squirrel at the same time. Luckily the trench coat stayed over both of them.

"**I will chase you back to your home!**" shouted Waldo.

"Huh?" said Becky. "That's not what you're supposed to do with stuffed animals. Also are you okay? Why are you on the floor?"

"I am from Liver, Ohio," said Waldo. "I WILL HAVE THAT SQUIRREL!"

"Wow," said Becky.

"What's happening?" said Stewart, who ran over as soon as he noticed Waldo on the floor, and stealthily helped him back up onto Sassy.

"SQUIRREL," said Waldo. "THERE WAS A SQUIRREL."

Two dozen guards ran over.

"Who is throwing items outside the gift shop?" asked one.

"You can throw things inside the gift shop but they can't land outside?" asked Stewart.

"It was a squirrel that escaped Squirreltown," said Waldo.

"We'll take it from here," said a guard, pulling out a net. "First we have to chase down two dogs, and now there's a squirrel loose? They're never going to believe this at guard school."

"It was a toy!" said Becky.

"Move along, move along, nothing to see here," said another guard.

The crowd of children made their way out of the gift shop.

"Okay! Children!" said Waldo, out of tour guide habit, and then realized he wasn't sure what to do next.

He looked out over the students, some of whom he knew, but many who were strangers. It made him a little uncomfortable, but was also exciting. He and Sassy were dogs of habit. But sometimes, it was okay to do something new. If you don't do a new thing, you can't lick a dinosaur. Benjamin Franklin probably said that, thought Waldo.

Waldo and Sassy weren't sure what to do next, but they had to do something.

"Follow me," said Waldo.

And they did.

CHAPTER SEVENTEEN

aldo and Sassy didn't know where they were going. They just knew they could smell a serene space, a space without so much three-hundred-year-old dust. They could smell white paint on the walls, and canvases painted black, and silence.

It was the modern art wing.

"This is some place completely different," Waldo told the crowd. Were there hundreds of children now? "This art likes it best if you whisper. Also do not squeeze any squirrels. Or if you do squeeze a squirrel, give it to me."

Waldo took out his index cards. This calm room was the perfect place to review the rules of the field trip.

"Yes, okay, so. Do not throw the art." Waldo shuffled through the index cards. "Do not go barefoot. Do not run. Do not leave **yogurt** on the windowsill. Do not fall asleep in outer space. Do not yell. Do not swim in the fountain. Do not touch the elephants. That's probably enough. Let's see what this is all about."

The dogs walked around the immense, spare room. It was a much better room for holding a tour group of this size than the gift shop had been. There were no distracting bins of squirrels. And the guards in this wing were aloof and unconcerned, like they were completely unaware of the kerfuffle the other guards were involved in.

They looked at a wall of huge paintings. These were not portraits of people. They were shapes.

The first was a big red circle.

"This is a beautiful painting of a **hamburger**," said Waldo.

The next was a yellow oval.

"This stunning painting is of a **hot dog** that has a lot of **mustard** on it," said Waldo. "Too much **mustard**? No, I think it's probably exactly the right amount of **mustard**."

"You're having **food** without me AGAIN?" asked Sassy.

"It is art!" said Waldo.

"Art is delicious," said Sassy.

They walked to a painting of an orange square.

"Oh, look!" said Bax. "**Cheese**!"

"That is right!" said Waldo. "Bax wins! It is such a nice painting of **cheese**."

"Technically, none of these are **food**," said Ralph. "This is the Forward Shapes series by Harriet Simon."

"Whatever you see in art is the right thing," said Waldo. "Maybe they are shapes to you, but they are **food** to me."

"I think they look like cat toys!" said a boy in the back.

"**Well, there's no way that's true**," said Waldo.

They moved on to a room of sculptures. One was a life-size car made out of clay, and Waldo and Sassy had to work very hard not to climb into the front seat and stick their heads out of the window.

They found a sculpture that was a miniature kick-ball game, re-created out of **bubble gum**, and everyone agreed it was very great art.

One modern art piece was a pile of soft fluffy yarn eight feet across and several feet high. Sassy felt it was an outrageous travesty that she had to walk past that one. It was clearly the world's best napping spot. That artist was a genius.

Waldo and Sassy loved the modern art. Everything was either **food** or a great place to nap. It was by far the most intriguing thing in the City Museum outside the dinosaurs and Squirreltown and the **food** court.

They had never thought about art this way. It had never occurred to them that art could be a well-dug hole or a perfectly constructed pile of **meat**. Waldo and Sassy liked coloring—they always had—but for the first time they wanted to make *art*. Something thought provoking. Something interesting. Something from deep within their souls.

Unfortunately, they didn't have a place to dig a hole or any **meat** to push into a pile. They had a bandana, an empty backpack, and index cards with rules on them.

It was worth a try.

Waldo dropped the cards on the floor. They made a satisfying swoosh noise. Some landed on top of each other, and some slid and fell farther away.

"What did you do that for?" asked Ralph.

"Art," said Waldo. "Also this **banana** makes me look jaunty."

"Huh?" said Ralph.

There was a murmuring commotion behind them.

"Exquisite."

"Radical."

"The juxtaposition of established rules and pop culture is a microcosm of modern life."

"Look at this one, the one that says, 'Don't throw **pudding**.' The blockiness of the letters versus the squishiness of the word '**pudding**' is incredible."

"A commentary on today's notions of societal norms. Truly groundbreaking. Where did this come from?"

"The fact that this piece is anonymous speaks to the larger themes."

Waldo cleared his throat. "This is *very good* art," he said. "The artist is clearly a very good artist."

"I would say that the artist has a phenomenal grasp of the interplay between lines and negative space," said a grown-up.

"Or that," said Waldo. "That also works."

"Look at you," said Stewart. "You're an artist."

"Do you think Ms. Twohey will be mad when she finds out I lost my index cards?"

"I doubt it."

Thinking about Ms. Twohey made Waldo very tired. It had been a long day. He loved school because Ms. Twohey and the other teachers told him what his job was. They gave him a list of things to do every day, and he did them, and if he did them right, he was a good dog, and sometimes they called him a star student or gave him a Good Job sticker, and that was the best. But today had been all about *Waldo* being a teacher, and he never realized how hard it was to teach all day. His feet hurt, and he wasn't even the one doing all the walking. It was hard to get this group of three hundred human children to focus on him and listen to him while he made up facts about the exhibits in the museum, or pointed out historical dogs that, inexplicably, no one else knew about.

"Stewart," said Waldo. "I want to go home now."

CHAPTER EIGHTEEN

Sassy walked slowly out of the modern art wing. She was tired too. So tired. It was time for them to find Ms. Twohey so she could nap on the bus and then nap at home and then eat dinner and then nap again until bedtime when she could finally sleep all night. She could barely stand up anymore.

There was something Waldo did sometimes when he was the top half of Salty. He didn't do it a lot. Only sometimes. It was a risky move, and usually when he did it, it wasn't exactly on purpose.

Sometimes Waldo closed his eyes and fell asleep.

He had enough practice balancing on top of Sassy that he could sway and shift while she walked, even if he was not entirely awake.

Waldo had the most wonderful nap. No one noticed. Arden started talking about how dogs can be trained to make coffee, and Ralph wanted to talk about how you can make paint out of muddled oak leaves.

Waldo woke with a start, and shouted the word "Hamburgasaur!"

Because there they were, finally. Back in the dinosaur room.

They were alone. Not even Stewart was with them.

"I think I am dreaming," said Sassy. "Because I do not see any humans. Only dinosaurs. So many dinosaurs. And no one here to tell us not to chew on them."

"If you are having that dream, then I am having the same dream," said Waldo.

"Just in case it's not a dream, we should lick all the dinosaurs we can right now," said Sassy.

"We should do that even if this *is* a dream," said Waldo.

There was yellow tape wrapped around poles blocking off the T. rex. The yellow tape had *Caution: Drool* written on it. The dogs went to the stegosaurus and blissfully tasted its leg, then munched on the troodon tail, and spent quality time investigating the ankylosaurus chin.

"I don't know why Stewart and all the other students said today would be dull," said Sassy, contemplatively licking the triceratops. "It's almost like they've never tasted dinosaur."

"I know," said Waldo, his mouth full of some kind of thigh bone, "it's like they're using the word *dull* wrong. Or . . . wait . . . are we using it wrong? Does it mean delicious ancient bones?"

"Maybe?" said Sassy, tasting each toe of the compsognathus. "Do you hear something?"

"Only the sound of us catching all these dinosaurs for dinner," said Waldo. "Wait, you're right, someone's coming. Quick, act natural!"

"Chewing on dinosaur bones is natural!" said Sassy.

"Act *human* natural."

"Oh."

Thirty-five museum security guards stormed into the room, carrying walkie-talkies, nets aloft, and shouting.

"We caught them! We caught them!" shouted one, seeing Salty leaning casually on a delicious-looking dinosaur tail, legs crossed, humming.

Waldo froze. Even he had to admit he looked pretty guilty, what with his slobber all over the dinosaur and extremely obvious lick marks on most of the fossils in the room. For once Sassy was glad to be hidden under the trench coat. Sure, if they got in trouble, it would be both of them—Salty—in trouble, but it would be Waldo's face in the mug shot when they were arrested.

The guards moved closer.

"Stay right there," said one.

Another raised a net high above her head and got ready to lower it over the dogs.

Sassy moved backward. Maybe there was still a way out. The guards were moving in, but they were human guards, burdened with equipment. Maybe there was a secret door under the apatosaurus. Maybe there was a trapdoor behind the diplodocus. Maybe there was a secret button that would make the dogs invisible.

"Waldo, I need you to distract the guards for a minute," said Sassy, who was inching along the wall toward the door. "I'm going to get us out of here."

"Distract them how?" asked Waldo.

"Distract who how?" said a guard. "Who are you talking to?"

"I am talking to you!" said Waldo. "I am Salty! I am from Liver, Ohio! Your museum is fun! I like the dinosaurs here, and all the many foods! I had astro-nut ice cream but it was like a food-flavored sponge! I think modern art is the best because it's all about snacking! Space is dark! Portraits are flat! Fountains are wet! Squirreltown is real!"

"That's perfect," whispered Sassy. Sassy got low on her belly. When Sassy got down this close to the ground, she knew she was invisible. Nobody could see her.

The guards looked on curiously, not understanding

why this kid had started crawling on the floor in the dinosaur room.

Slowly, the guards made a U formation around the slinking dogs.

"Sassy, what are you doing? It's not workingggg," said Waldo.

"Shhh, they can't see me when I do this," whispered Sassy.

"Yeah, but they can see me," said Waldo. "**Don't mind me, guards, I'm just stretching out after a long day of museum learning.**"

The guards were upon them immediately.

CHAPTER NINETEEN

A ha!" yelled a guard. "Got you!"

"Just what in the tiddly toodly world do you all think you're doing?" said a voice. Waldo looked behind him to see who it was.

"Gordy! The tour guide!" said Waldo. "I am so glad to see you!"

"What do you mean, silly billy?" said Gordy. "You've been seeing me the whole ding-dang day while I did the *incredibly important* work of guiding you around this here educational institution!"

"Oh, yes!" said Waldo. "That is correct!"

"Hi there, Salty," said Ms. Twohey. "Are you okay? Why are you on the floor?"

Sassy stood up.

"I am fine. How are you? Have you had a fun day? Does Stewart get a sticker?" asked Waldo.

"Oh, I'm having a great day, of course! It's City Museum day!" Ms. Twohey moved between Salty and the guards and started to shoo them away. "Thanks for your, uh, help. Looks like Salty's just fine! Not sure why so many of you had to rush over."

"I know you don't think I can handle a large group of children, but I most definitely can," said Gordy. "You can go now."

The guards did not go. They did not look happy.

"Here is Stewart and all my other friends!" said Waldo. The non-Bea-Arthur students had found their own teacher and gone back to their own school. "What time is it? Have we been here all week? Is it midnight?"

"Not quite," said Ms. Twohey, "but it is almost time to go home. As Gordy said just a few minutes ago when we were at the Viking longboat, which for some reason you don't remember, we're headed down to the Hall of Enormity to discuss all the things we learned today."

One of the guards tapped Gordy on the shoulder. "After your little conclusionary talk, we're going to have to take that kid there down to the guard room for questioning."

"I don't think that sounds fun at all," said Waldo. "Maybe I will have to go home first forever."

One of the guards looked at Waldo. "Listen, little school kid, we know you witnessed something today. We've been on the case all afternoon. Your group has left every room just before we discovered some new evidence. We just need you to describe the misbehaving dogs to our forensic sketch artist. It'll be okay. We won't hurt the pups."

"That's impossible," Ms. Twohey chimed in. "We've all been together this whole day."

"Technically—" said Ralph.

"Of course we've been together all day," said Stewart.

"All day?" asked the guard. "You're saying these students have been with you all day? And you haven't seen two dogs running around here, licking, and chewing, and drooling?"

"Certainly not. We've had a totally educational day so far!" said Ms. Twohey, twirling in delight. "I can't believe how much

we've all learned! Well, I can. It's the same amount we learn every year. Which is a lot."

"A full day with Cap'n Talky here? That's its own punishment," said the guard.

"Who's Cap'n Talky?" asked Arden.

"That guy," said the guard, pointing at Gordy.

"You don't know each other's names?" said Stewart. "You've all worked here for years."

"Well, sure, but because of the guards versus guides rivalry, we just make up nicknames for all the guides," said the guard.

"We do the same thing," said Gordy. "We call you Joe **Bananas**, because you're always eating **bananas**."

"Somebody finally got a **banana**?" Sassy whispered.

"They're an important source of potassium," said the guard.

"I'm not going to argue with you there," said Gordy.

"What is your actual human name, Joe Bananas?" asked Waldo.

"It's Gerard," said the guard.

"Gerard the guard, meet Gordy the guide," said Waldo. "See? You are shaking hands. That is nice. No one has to go to jail today."

"I like **bananas** too," said Gordy.

"I am embarrassed I never looked at you as anything more than Cap'n Talky," said Gerard.

"I do talk a lot!" said Gordy.

"Do you want to go eat **bananas** in the atrium?" asked Gerard.

"You bet I do, Joe Ban—Gerard," said Gordy.

"And I suppose since you all say you were together this whole day and nobody saw any dogs, that's good enough for me. I trust your teacher. You're all free to go," said Gerard.

"But, Gordy, what about the talk you were going to give us all in the Hall of Enormity?" asked Ms. Twohey.

"Oh, you can do that for me," said Gordy. "You know as well as I do what all the factoids and educational bits and bobs of the day were!"

"But I like when you talk," said Ms. Twohey.

"I have to go eat a **banana** with my new friend, Gerard! You kidderoonies were so great today! So quiet! Goodbye all of you! See you next year!"

"See you next year!" said Waldo. "I hope none of us gets turned into statues!"

And with that Gordy and Gerard went to the atrium to eat **bananas**.

$\mathcal{D}$oes anyone want to talk about what you learned today?" asked Ms. Twohey when they got to the Hall of Enormity. "What was your favorite part? I'll start: My favorite part was discussing thread counts and weave structures in the tapestry room. So fascinating!"

"It was cool running around like that painting," said Bax.

"I can't wait to get home and do more research on Squirreltown," said Becky.

"I'm going to watch every Sergeant Barkles movie," said Arden. "That was the best part of the tour."

"I liked when Salty made modern art," said Ralph.

"Listen to all of you, so full of imagination!" said Ms. Twohey. "I've never seen a group of students so energized after a day at the museum! Maybe we should come back more often."

Everyone groaned.

"MS. Twohey, we had fun at the museum, but when we are at the museum, we are not learning in your amazing classroom, and that makes us sad," said Waldo.

"Oh, you," said Ms. Twohey.

Ms. Twohey made everyone line up and head out to the parking lot to find the bus. Waldo and Sassy breathed in deeply. The outside air smelled great after being in the museum all day.

As soon as they were on the bus, Sassy lay down and started snoring (luckily, the sound of her snores was drowned out by the bus engine).

"Today sure was an exciting day," said Waldo. "You said it was going to be boring, Stewart, but it was not."

"Thanks to you," said Stewart.

Ms. Twohey stood up at the front of the bus.

"What a wonderful day, everyone! I really appreciate how attentive and respectful you all were. As a reward, you are all going to get a Good Job sticker."

"Yay! Stewart!" said Waldo. "You can get your shiny, pretty pencil!"

"And also, here is the big surprise. Remember I promised you an **ice cream** party? We're going to have it on the bus ride home. I got astronaut **ice cream** for everyone! You may not have had this before, but it's something very different."

Ms. Twohey walked up and down the aisle, passing out the silvery packets of astronaut **ice cream**.

"I got **Vanilla Shooting Star**," Waldo told Stewart. "It tastes like someone waved a **cookie** in the air and then made that smell solid."

"Do you like it?" asked Stewart.

"I think it is terrible," said Waldo.

Sassy woke up suddenly. "What is terrible? I smell **foodish** smells. Not **food** exactly, but . . . what is that? Do you have **food** up there?"

"We got **ice cream**!" said Waldo.

"Yay!" said Sassy.

"Astronaut **ice cream**," said Stewart.

"Boo," said Sassy. "But hand me some anyway."

Ms. Twohey went back to the front of the bus and sat down, and the bus driver pulled away, driving back toward Bea Arthur Elementary. Waldo heard someone yelling and turned to see three museum guards running after the bus. One of them was waving some papers in his hand.

"You charged over five hundred dollars in the **food** court!" he yelled. "Come back!"

"That would probably be important if I hadn't eaten that rule," said Waldo.

The bus drove into the Bea Arthur parking lot. Coach was waiting for them, and blew on his whistle as the bus rumbled to a stop. The students tumbled out and gathered their bags to go home.

As soon as Stewart and the dogs were out of sight of the school, Waldo hopped off Sassy and stretched. Sassy shimmied back and forth, glad to be able to move more now that Waldo wasn't balancing on top of her.

"I am a dog," said Waldo.

"Yeah, I know," said Stewart, smiling.

"Dogs do not like change," said Waldo.

"That's true," said Sassy.

"Today was a lot," said Waldo. "It was so much change. School has been a change."

"A fun change though, right?" said Stewart.

"Oh, yes! We get **lunch** now, and that's very fun," said Waldo. "Also Ms. Twohey is nice, and all our new friends are great."

"But we are still adjusting to going to school," said Sassy. "We had our other routine for *years*."

"What are you getting at?" asked Stewart.

"I liked chewing on the dinosaur, but I cannot go on another field trip tomorrow," said Waldo.

"Tomorrow will be a regular day at school," said Stewart.

"It will?" asked Waldo. "A regular day, with math and spelling and gym class?"

"And napping under the desk?" asked Sassy.

"That's right," said Stewart.

"That's a relief," said Sassy.

"Do you think it'll be okay if I wear this **banana** every day?" said Waldo. "To show my Bea Arthur pride. And also because I look so very jaunty."

"Yup," said Stewart, and he took off his own bandana and tied it around Sassy's neck.

"Now we're both jaunty," said Sassy, and they went home and slept for fifteen hours.

Julie Falatko is the author of Snappsy the Alligator series, illustrated by Tim Miller; *No Boring Stories*, illustrated by Charles Santoso; and *The Great Indoors*, illustrated by Ruth Chan. Julie lives in Maine with her family, including her two dogs, and loves to make everyone (except the dogs) go to museums. To learn more about Julie, please visit juliefalatko.com.

Colin Jack is the illustrator of a number of books for children including *If You Happen to Have a Dinosaur, Under-the-Bed Fred, 1 Zany Zoo*, and the Galaxy Zack series. He also works as a story artist and character designer in the animation industry and has been involved in the production of *Hotel Transylvania, The Book of Life, The Boss Baby*, and *Captain Underpants: The First Epic Movie*. Born in Vancouver, Colin currently resides in California with his wife and two sons.

Sassy and Waldo are good dogs.

And these loyal pups need to save their boy,
Stewart, but the school won't let two dogs insid
Good thing they found that trench coat!

★ "With plenty of comical reinforcement from Jack's
freewheeling sketches, Falatko spins this promising
premise into a hilarious romp."
—*Booklist*, starred review